The Monster Squad

ALSO IN THE JUNIOR MONSTER SCOUTS SERIES

JUNIOR MONSTER SCOUTS

#1 The Monster Squad

By Joe McGee
Illustrated by Ethan Long

ALADDIN
NEW YORK   LONDON   TORONTO   SYDNEY   NEW DELHI

ALADDIN

An imprint of Simon & Schuster Children's Publishing Division
1230 Avenue of the Americas, New York, New York 10020
First Aladdin paperback edition September 2019
Text copyright © 2019 by Joseph McGee
Illustrations copyright © 2019 by Ethan Long
Also available in an Aladdin hardcover edition.
All rights reserved, including the right of reproduction in whole or in part in any form.
ALADDIN and related logo are registered trademarks of Simon & Schuster, Inc.
For information about special discounts for bulk purchases, please contact Simon & Schuster Special Sales at 1-866-506-1949 or business@simonandschuster.com.
The Simon & Schuster Speakers Bureau can bring authors to your live event.
For more information or to book an event contact the Simon & Schuster Speakers Bureau at 1-866-248-3049 or visit our website at www.simonspeakers.com.
Cover designed by Karin Paprocki
Interior designed by Mike Rosamilia
The illustrations for this book were rendered digitally.
The text of this book was set in Centaur MT.
Manufactured in the United States of America 0620 OFF
4 6 8 10 9 7 5 3
Library of Congress Control Number 2019931561
ISBN 978-1-5344-3677-0 (hc)
ISBN 978-1-5344-3676-3 (pbk)
ISBN 978-1-5344-3678-7 (eBook)

FOR JESSICA

★ ★ ★ ★

*I will not let you go into
the unknown alone.*
—Bram Stoker

· THE SCOUTS ·

VAMPYRA may be a vampire, but that doesn't mean she wants your blood. Gross! In fact, she doesn't even like ketchup! She loves gymnastics, especially cart-wheels, and one of her favorite things is hanging upside down . . . even when she's not a bat. She loves garlic in her food and sleeps in past noon, preferring the nighttime over the day. She lives in Castle Dracula with her mom, dad (Dracula), and aunts, who are always after her to brush her fangs and clean her cape.

WOLFY and his family live high in the mountains above Castle Dracula, where they can get the best view of the moon. He likes to hike and play in the creek and gaze at the stars. He especially likes to fetch sticks with his dad, Wolf Man, and go on family pack runs, even if he has to put up with all of his little brothers and sisters. They're always howling when he tries to talk! Mom says he has his father's fur. Boy, is he proud of that!

FRANKY STEIN has always been bigger than the other monsters. But it's not just his body that's big. It's his brain and his heart as well. He has plenty of hugs and smiles to go around. His dad, Frankenstein, is the scout-master, and one of Franky's favorite things is his well-worn Junior Monster Scout handbook. One day Franky is going to be a scoutmaster, like his dad. But for now . . . he wants a puppy. Dad says he'll make Franky one soon. Mom says Franky has to keep his workshop clean for a week first.

GLOOMY
WOODS

LAKE

VILLAGE

BARON VON
GRUMP'S HOUSE

1

WOLFY TOOK A DEEP BREATH. HE LOOKED to the sky. He leaned way back and let out the biggest, longest, loudest howl he could. It was a very good howl. It was such a good howl that it went right past the forest, over the covered bridge, through the village, and all the way to the Old Windmill.

"That was a good one!" said Franky Stein.

"I'll bet they could hear that howl all the way back at the castle!" said Vampyra.

"Thanks!" said Wolfy. He was very proud of himself. Tonight was the Junior Monster Scout meeting, and Wolfy wanted to earn his Howling Merit Badge.

In fact, Wolfy's howl was such a good howl that it reached right through the open window of the Old Windmill, right into the ears of Baron Von Grump.

Baron Von Grump was always grumpy. Everything about him was grumpy. Even his eyebrows were grumpy. They were like two big, black, bushy, *grumpy* caterpillars crawling across his forehead. They were even blacker than Edgar, his pet crow.

"What was that *noise*?" he sneered. "That sounded like a howl. A *monstrous* howl. Oh, how I despise those wretched monsters!"

Edgar hopped onto the windowsill and peered out over the village. "Caw, caw!" Edgar did not like monsters either.

Baron Von Grump did not like noise. Baron Von Grump did not like anything, really, except for playing his violin and making plans. Baron Von Grump *loved* making plans. He loved that almost as much as he loved playing his violin.

So you see, Baron Von Grump loved *two* things. And everything else, he did not. Okay, he loved Edgar, too. *Three* things. Baron Von Grump loved three things.

Baron Von Grump looked out his window and glared at the village. Edgar glared with him.

Today was the village cheese festival, and all of the villagers were busy setting up.

"Look at them!" he said. "Smiling, talking, singing, why . . . they're even chewing gum! I cannot stand when people chew gum . . . or sing, or talk, or smile. These villagers are almost as bad as those miserable monsters."

See? Baron Von Grump did not like anything besides making plans and his violin and Edgar. With all of this noise Baron Von Grump could not concentrate. If he could not concentrate, he could not play his violin. If he could not play his violin, he would become even grumpier than the grump he already was. And *that* is a *lot* of grump.

"I have a plan!" he said with a sly smirk.

"Caw! Caw!" said Edgar.

A plan! This made Baron Von Grump happy for one half of a second.

Make a smile. Just a little one. Barely twitch the corners of your mouth. Now stop. That was how long Baron Von Grump was happy. That was not very long, was it?

Edgar hopped onto Baron Von Grump's shoulder.

Baron Von Grump slammed his shutters closed. He knew just what to do to get rid of all of those smiling, talking, singing, gum-chewing villagers. He knew just how to chase them away.

JUST AS WOLFY WAS GETTING READY to howl again, he heard something. He stopped. He listened. Wolfy was a very good listener. He had ears like a wolf.

It sounded like someone was crying. It did not sound like a good cry, like when you get a new puppy or some ice cream and you're so happy that you cry. No, this sounded like a sad cry.

"Hey," said Wolfy, "I hear someone."

Wolfy followed the sound of crying. Vampyra and Franky went with him. The crying led them down past the graveyard, along the crooked trail, and right to the edge of the Gloomy Woods. A little boy sat by the side of the trail. It was Peter, the piper, from the village. He was crying into his hat.

"What's wrong?" asked Wolfy.

Peter jumped. "Don't eat me!"

The junior monsters looked confused.

Stop reading and look at the nearest person. Now say, "Don't eat me!" They look confused, don't they? They are probably giving you a funny look. That is the kind of look the junior monsters gave Peter.

"Why would we eat you?" asked Vampyra.

"Because you're monsters," said Peter. "Monsters eat people, right?"

"We're friendly monsters," said Franky.

"Friendly monsters?" Peter asked. "The stories don't say anything about *friendly* monsters."

"That's just it," said Vampyra. She swished her cape. "They're only *stories!*"

"My dad says Baron Von Grump made up all of those stories about us," said Franky. "And everyone believed him."

"Well, you're certainly not scary, like in the stories," said Peter. "I've never met a real monster before."

"We're not just monsters. We are Junior Monster *Scouts*!" said Wolfy. "Why are you crying?"

"I was playing a song on my flute, and when I turned around, my Shadow was gone!" Peter said.

"Cheer up," said Franky. "We'll find your shadow!" He looked behind a bush. He looked under a rock. "Have you checked your pockets? Oh, hey, I found it! Look, there it is!" He pointed to Peter's shadow stretched out next to him.

"Not *that* shadow," said Peter. "My kitten. *Her* name is Shadow." He started to cry again.

Peter was very sad.

Wolfy, Vampyra, and Franky did not like seeing anyone sad.

"Don't worry," said Wolfy. "We'll help you find Shadow."

"You will?" said Peter. He wiped his tears away.

"We sure will," said Franky.

"By paw or claw, by tooth or wing, Junior Monster Scouts can do anything!" said Vampyra.

"WE'LL FIND SHADOW BY FOLLOWING her scent," said Wolfy. He pointed to his nose. "I am very good at sniffing things out."

"Shadow likes to sleep in my hat," said Peter. "Maybe that will help."

Wolfy sniffed Peter's hat. He sniffed the air. He sniffed the ground. He sniffed the air again.

"Do you have anything that belongs to Shadow?" asked Wolfy.

"I have her favorite toy," said Peter. He held out a little stuffed mouse.

Wolfy sniffed that, too. "Aha!" he said.

He had Shadow's scent, and he had the trail. But he did not like where it led.

"Shadow went in there," he said. He pointed to the Gloomy Woods.

Peter gulped.

Franky shivered.

Vampyra squeezed her eyes shut.

The Gloomy Woods was dark, and spooky, and very, very gloomy. That's why it was called the Gloomy Woods.

You might think that monsters would like dark, spooky, and very, very gloomy things. But that is just another *story*. They only like kind of gloomy things, not very, *very* gloomy.

"It won't be so bad if we go in together," said Wolfy. He took one step toward the woods. He was nervous.

"I have an idea," said Vampyra. "I know a way to make the Gloomy Woods not so gloomy."

"How?" asked Franky. "I don't think anything can make it less gloomy."

"Peter," said Vampyra, "did you say you play the flute?"

"I do," said Peter. "I can play lots of songs!"

"Well, then why don't you play us a song?" asked Vampyra.

Peter picked up his flute and played a song. It was a cheery, happy song. It worked! They all felt a little better, a

little braver, and a lot less gloomy.

"Lead the way, Peter!" said Franky.

Wolfy, Franky, and Vampyra followed
Peter into the Gloomy Woods.

BARON VON GRUMP COVERED HIS EARS. He growled. He groaned. He grimaced. *Why is everyone so loud? And happy?* Why, he'd even heard a villager say "Good morning" to another villager just a minute ago.

Every villager was out and about, young and old, waving their little cheese flags, and wearing hats made of cheese wheels. There was even a parade and a wagon piled high with cheese. White cheese, yellow cheese, pink cheese, cheese with holes. Square cheese, round cheese. Cheese, cheese, cheese, CHEESE!

"They are driving me crazy with all of their noise!" he said to Edgar. "How am I supposed to practice my violin with them making such a racket? And oh, the stench! The horrible, terrible stink of their cheeses."

Baron Von Grump pinched his nose shut with a clothespin. "Bud I hab a plan. I doh justh whut to do!"

"Caw! Caw!" said Edgar.

Baron Von Grump went down, down, down the sagging staircase of the Old Windmill, all the way to the basement. Edgar flew down the stairs, leading the way. Baron Von Grump hardly ever went down to the basement. He lived in the top room of the very old, very rickety, very crooked windmill. The basement was dark, and damp, and filled with rats. Big, hairy black rats with long pink tails and bright red eyes.

Baron Von Grump lit a candle. The rats blinked. There were a lot of rats. There was a lot of blinking.

"Hey," said a very big rat, munching on a wedge of cheese, "put that candle out!"

The rats did not like light very much.

"How would you like all the cheese you could eat?" asked Baron Von Grump.

The rats liked cheese a lot. They liked cheese *more* than they disliked light. The

rats listened to what Baron Von Grump had to say. Baron Von Grump said that there was a lot of cheese in the village. He said that each house was filled with cheese. He also said that the rats could have *all* of it . . . as long as they chased the villagers away. And chewed their cheese *quietly*.

"Hmm," said the big rat. "I'll put it to a vote."

The big rat called all of the other rats together and explained Baron Von Grump's offer. The rats thought this was a very good idea. Unfortunately, the village was much brighter than the basement of the Old Windmill, but the village was also filled with cheese.

"We'll do it!" said the big rat. He swallowed his wedge of cheese. He burped. He did not have very nice manners.

Baron Von Grump smiled. It was a very small smile, a crooked smile, certainly not a full smile. But it was something.

Edgar's beady little black eyes seemed to smile as well.

"Soon," said Baron Von Grump, "those villagers will be gone, and I'll finally have some peace and quiet. I will finally be able to play my violin without all of their cheering and chattering and cheese stink!"

CHAPTER

5

CHAPTER

5

THE GLOOMY WOODS WAS VERY, VERY dark. It was so dark that Wolfy, Vampyra, Franky, and Peter could barely see their own hands in front of their own faces.

The Gloomy Woods was also filled with trees. Lots and lots of trees to walk right into. Or roots to trip you up. The Gloomy Woods was a dangerous place.

"Ouch!" said Peter. A branch knocked his hat off.

"Oof!" said Franky. He stumbled over a log.

Wolfy and Vampyra did not stumble or hit anything. Werewolves and vampires can see in the dark. But that did not help Peter and Franky.

"We need to help them," said Vampyra.

"We can be their eyes," said Wolfy.

Wolfy held Peter's hand. Vampyra held Franky's hand. Now they could walk through the Gloomy Woods.

Wolfy sniffed the air.

"Shadow is close!" he said.

"She might be scared of you at first, like I was," said Peter.

"She might hide from us," said Franky.

"I think Peter can help with that," said Vampyra. "His music helped us feel not so

gloomy. Maybe he can help Shadow feel not so gloomy."

"Good idea," said Peter. He took out his flute and played another song.

When he was finished with his song, he put his flute away. The junior monsters waited and listened. A soft meow came from somewhere in front of them. In front of them and *above* them.

"Did you hear something?" asked Franky.

"That's Shadow!" said Peter.

"Meow!"

"Shadow is in one of these trees!" said Wolfy.

"Which one?" Peter asked. But he could not even see one tree, let alone the tree that Shadow was in. Close your eyes. Close them tight. Now look for a kitten. You can't see one, right? You can't see anything. That's how dark it was.

"I think I know a way to find out which tree Shadow is in," said Vampyra.

CHAPTER

6

THE VILLAGE WAS FILLED WITH RATS.

Big rats, short rats, thin rats, long rats. Rats scampered down the streets. They crawled into houses through windows. They slid under doors. They hopped onto roofs and dropped down the chimneys. They twitched their pink tails and grinned with their yellow teeth. The rats ran *everywhere* . . . and everywhere they ran, the villagers ran too.

"This is great!" said the rats. "So much cheese!"

Now, mind you, the rats were not hurting anyone. They certainly did not want to *overly* upset the villagers. All they wanted was cheese, and Baron Von Grump had been right. There was a lot of cheese in this village! But the villagers did not know what the rats wanted. The villagers did not stop to ask the rats why they had come in through the windows and down the chimneys, and why they were on the village streets.

The villagers just ran in circles. They climbed atop wagons. They stood on chairs.

"There are too many of them!" said a villager.

"We'll never get rid of them all!" said another.

"They're eating our cheese!" cried a third villager.

"Everyone!" said the mayor, shouting through a very loud bullhorn. "Gather your things. Pack your bags. Collect your children. We must leave the village!"

Baron Von Grump clapped his hands together. He leaned out of his window and watched.

"My plan is working!" he said. "Soon those cheese-eating, song-singing, gum-chewing, happy villagers will be gone and I'll be able to play, play, play my violin without any distraction!"

He spun in a circle, jumped up, and clicked his heels together. Edgar sat on the edge of a rafter and bobbed his head up and down.

"Caw! Caw!"

"Yes, my friend," said Baron Von Grump, "the sooner the better." He did not like the villagers' panicked hollering and shouting, and he certainly did not like the mayor's bullhorn.

Baron Von Grump slammed his shutters closed again. He stomped to his favorite chair, sat down, and opened his violin case. He blew off the dust and the cobwebs and lifted the violin to his chin.

He placed the bow on the strings.

He took a deep breath, closed his eyes, and drew the bow across the strings.

It made a terrible screech.

"Caw! Caw!" shrieked Edgar. He flew straight to the window . . . and into the closed shutters.

"Well, of course it's not tuned!" growled Baron Von Grump, waving his bow. "How

am I supposed to tune it when I can't even hear myself think?!"

Edgar shrugged his wings. Baron Von Grump shoved his violin back into the case and slapped the lid closed.

CHAPTER

7

SINCE VAMPYRA WAS A VAMPIRE, SHE had a few special powers. One of her powers was being able to turn into a bat. If Vampyra turned into a bat, she could see better in the dark *and* she could fly up to the tops of the trees to see which one Shadow was in.

Wolfy, Franky, and Peter thought this was a very good idea.

"Meow."

So did Shadow.

Vampyra closed her eyes. She wrapped her cape around her body. She counted, "One . . . two . . . three." And then POOF! Vampyra turned into a bat.

She fluttered and flapped and flittered around the others. Being a bat was fun! She was close to earning her Junior Monster Scout Flying Merit Badge.

"Do you see her yet?" asked Peter.

"Not yet!" said Vampyra.

Vampyra flew up above their heads. She flew higher and higher, and soon she was at the top branches. It was even darker up there! There were lots of branches and lots of leaves.

But as a bat, Vampyra could see even better.

"Meow, meow," said Shadow.

Vampyra was getting close. She soared and swooped and flew around the branches and treetops.

"I see her!" she said. Vampyra flapped her wings and got closer. Sure enough, Shadow was curled up on a branch right over their heads. "You certainly do look like a shadow," Vampyra said to the little black kitten. "I almost didn't see you."

Shadow arched her back and stared at Vampyra the bat, and then at the ground. She hissed. She blinked her green eyes. She wanted to jump, but it was too far and she was scared.

"It's okay," said Vampyra. She flashed her best batty smile. "We'll help you get down."

"Meow, meow."

Vampyra flapped back down to her friends. She fluttered in the air, and her wings became her cape, and one . . . two . . . three . . . her body changed from bat to girl.

"Wow!" said Peter. "I wish I could do that!"

"Did you find her?" asked Wolfy.

"I did," said Vampyra. "Shadow is right above us. But it's too far for her to jump, too high for us to reach, and I'm too little a bat to carry her."

Franky scratched his head. He twisted his bolts. He'd listened hard to what Vampyra had said. Franky was a very good listener.

"Too high to reach?" he asked.

"I'm afraid so," said Vampyra.

"Maybe not for *all* of us," said Franky.

CHAPTER
8

BARON VON GRUMP WAITED. HE LISTENED. He waited and listened. No one was hollering. No one was shouting. No one was singing or saying, "Good morning." No one was shouting, "RATS!" And there was certainly no bullhorn.

"Could it be?" asked Baron Von Grump. "Could those irksome villagers finally be gone?"

"Caw, caw!" said Edgar.

"Yes! Yes, my fine feathered friend," said Baron Von Grump, "let us see for ourselves."

He stomped over to his shutters. He pushed them wide open. He raised his big,

black, bushy eyebrows. And then Baron Von Grump did something that Baron Von Grump rarely ever did.

Baron Von Grump smiled. Not a small, crooked smile like before. This was a full, wide, genuine smile.

He looked to the left. He looked to the right. He looked across the village.

"They're gone!" he said. He clapped his hands together and danced in a little circle. "The villagers have all gone. My rat plan was a success!"

There were no villagers. No horses. No wagons. No children. No chickens. No smiling or singing or gum-chewing or "good mornings." The village was entirely empty . . . except for the rats.

Big, fat, lazy rats with wedges of cheese, as far as the eye could see.

Baron Von Grump leaned out his window and shouted down to the rats, "Hey! Would you mind nibbling your cheese just a bit more *quietly?*"

"Sure thing, boss," said the big rat. "HEY! RATS! QUIET DOWN!"

Baron Von Grump's smile disappeared. Rats had been part of his plan. *Loud*, nibbling, cheese-chomping rats had not.

CHAPTER
9

FRANKY STRETCHED HIS LONG ARMS. He stretched his long legs. He stood on his tippy toes and felt around. His fingers touched the bottom branch, but Shadow was still too high up.

Stand up and stretch as high as you can. Put your arms way up over your head. Now wiggle your fingers about. Can you feel a kitten? No, you cannot. That's how Franky felt.

"We'll never be able to reach her," said Peter.

"Never say 'never' when friends work together!" said Franky. "Wolfy, climb onto my shoulders."

Wolfy climbed up and reached for Shadow. But they were still not high enough.

"Vampyra, can you climb onto Wolfy's shoulders?" asked Franky.

Vampyra climbed up. But they were still not tall enough.

"We're so close!" said Vampyra.

"Okay, Peter. Your turn," said Franky. "Be careful!"

"But it's so high up!" said Peter.

"I'll hold your legs," said Vampyra.

"And I'll keep us steady," said Franky.

"We won't let you fall," said Wolfy. "A Junior Monster Scout is always careful and kind."

"Well, okay, then," said Peter. He climbed

up Franky, up Wolfy, and up onto Vampyra's shoulders.

"A little to the left," said Peter. "A little more. Almost there . . ."

Peter's fingers touched soft fur.

"That's it!" said Peter.

"Meow," said Shadow.

Peter gently lifted Shadow off the branch and climbed back down.

He stepped off Vampyra's shoulders and onto Wolfy's head.

"Owwwww!" howled Wolfy.

"Sorry!" Peter said.

Shadow squirmed in Peter's hand.

Peter stepped off Wolfy's head and onto Franky's bolts.

"Yeowch!" Franky hollered.

"Didn't mean that," said Peter.

Shadow arched her back. Peter held her tight and slid down off Franky.

"That was a challenge!" Peter said.

"You're telling me," grumbled Wolfy, rubbing his head.

Once they were all back on the ground, the black kitten jumped right onto Peter's head and curled up under his hat.

"I'm so glad you're safe, Shadow!" said Peter. "I was scared that you'd stay lost."

"Meow," said Shadow. She had been scared too.

But they were still in the Gloomy Woods, and that made them *all* a little scared.

"Maybe we should get out of here," said Wolfy.

Everyone thought that was a very good idea.

Since Wolfy and Vampyra could see better in the dark, they led the group out of the Gloomy Woods. It felt good to be back in the sun, even for Vampyra, who preferred to sleep in during the day and stay up later at night.

But little did they know that while they'd been helping Peter to rescue Shadow, things had gone crazy in the village!

Peter and the Junior Monster Scouts could not believe what they saw. Everyone was leaving the village! Horses and wagons and people with packs and bags and baskets and suitcases marched down the road *away* from the village and away from the Gloomy Woods and the Junior Monster Scouts. They were taking the road toward the lake, and they were sure in a hurry. It was a long, long line of frantic villagers, with the mayor at the front, leading them all with his bullhorn, on his bicycle.

"Hurry!" the mayor shouted through his bullhorn. "Run! Run for your lives! Orderly running, please. No pushing or shoving!"

But everyone pushed and shoved. They were running for their lives!

(Which is kind of silly because the rats weren't hurting anyone at all.)

"Where is everyone going?" asked Wolfy.

"I don't know," said Peter. "Today is the village cheese festival! Let's go find out."

"But they're all the way down the road," said Vampyra.

"We'll never catch them!" said Franky.

"And the mayor's bullhorn is so loud," said Peter. "They won't hear us calling them."

Shadow wiggled out from under Peter's hat. She landed on her feet (cats always land on their feet) and curled around Vampyra's legs.

"I think she likes you," said Peter.

Then Shadow arched her back, straightened her tail, and let out the loudest "Meow" she could. It was very tiny and very cute, but not loud enough to be heard over the shouting, pushing, shoving, and bullhorn.

However, it *did* give Wolfy an idea.

"That's it!" said Wolfy. "Thanks, Shadow! I

know just how to get the villagers' attention."

Wolfy leaned way, way, way back and let out the loudest howl he could.

It worked! The villagers stopped pushing and shoving, and the mayor rode his bicycle back to Peter and the Junior Monster Scouts.

"Where is everyone going?" Peter asked.

The mayor explained the rat problem to them. "And so you see," said the mayor, "we have to leave. They're everywhere! Nibbling our crackers, chomping our cheese, jumping onto our pillows, and climbing our walls. There are too many of them. We have no choice! Oh, woe is us!"

Peter held up his flute.

"I think we might be able to help," he said.

CHAPTER
10

PETER'S PLAN WAS SIMPLE.

First they brought Shadow into the village. As soon as she crawled out from under Peter's hat, she saw the rats. And the rats saw her. Rats do not like kittens. Kittens do not like rats.

Of course, there were other cats in the village. But the village cats were old, and lazy, and not at all interested in chasing around big, cheese-eating rats. Not when the cats could curl up in the sun and swish their tails about.

But Shadow was young, and full of energy, and *very* much interested in chasing a bunch of cheese-eating rats.

The rats dropped their cheese wedges. Shadow hissed. The rats shrieked. Baron Von Grump had *not* mentioned anything about a kitten to the rats. He had promised cheese, and lots of it. But he had failed to mention anything about a spitting, biting, scratching kitten. And what if she woke up the rest of the older lazy, napping cats? What then? No way!

"Run for your lives!" the big rat yelled. Then he burped. He really didn't have any manners at all.

Rats hopped out of windows. They scurried up chimneys. They ran under doors and along rooftops. Everywhere they ran, Shadow followed, darting left and right, right and left. She chased them all in one direction . . . *out* of the village.

Shadow did not really want to catch any of the rats. This was just a fun game for her. But the rats didn't know this, and the rats were scared. There was a lot of pushing and shoving as the rats fled for their lives.

"I feel bad for them," said Wolfy. "All they wanted was cheese."

"They look pretty scared," said Vampyra.

"I have an idea," said Franky. He leaned over and whispered into Peter's ear.

Franky was not telling secrets. That would have been rude. Rats have very good hearing, and Franky didn't want the rats to know what the Junior Monster Scouts were up to. Franky was quite clever.

Peter grinned. "That is a very good idea," he said.

He picked up his flute and played. It was a happy song. It was the kind of song that might make you think of ice cream, and your favorite toy, and warm, fuzzy blankets. When the rats heard it, they felt happy. Very happy. Even the big, burping rat with no manners was happy.

The rats were so happy that they stopped running. They stopped pushing and shoving. They formed one line of happy, smiling rats, following Peter and his flute.

"It's working!" said Wolfy.

"But where should we lead them?" Franky asked. "Where can *they* be happy too?"

"I know!" said Vampyra. "There's plenty of

room in the castle! I'm sure my mom and dad won't mind. We have a great big basement with more than enough room for all of these rats. They can even have Ping-Pong tournaments!"

Peter played his flute and followed Vampyra, Franky, and Wolfy to Dracula's castle. The rats followed Peter. Shadow followed the rats. It was a very long line.

They crossed the drawbridge over the moat. They marched into the castle. They went down, down, down into the basement. Then Peter stopped playing.

"Here you go," said Vampyra to the rats. "You can stay here for as long as you like."

She was right. There was lots of room! And lots of dark places and lots of

cobwebs. It was perfect for a rat.

"Thank you!" said the big rat.

Well, maybe he had *some* manners.

"What's this? What's going on?" said Vampyra's dad from the basement steps.

"Where did all these rats come from?"

"From the village," said Franky.

"They needed a place to stay," said Wolfy, "and they can't stay in the village."

"And our basement is so big," said Vampyra. "Please, Dad? Please, can they stay?"

"Well, I don't see why not," said Vampyra's dad. "But no scampering around at all hours of the day!" he said to the rats. "I need my beauty sleep."

"You—you're *Dracula*," said Peter. "Like, in the stories. You're a *real* monster!"

"What? No!" said Dracula. He popped out one of his pointy teeth. "These aren't even real. See?" He waved it around. "Fake!"

"Then why do you wear them?" Peter asked.

Dracula shrugged. "Good question."

CHAPTER 11

BARON VON GRUMP'S SMILE HAD GONE from a big grin to a little twitch, to a thin line, to a frown. A full, frumpy, sour frown.

Baron Von Grump was angry. He was so angry that he hopped up and down. He stomped his feet. He wrinkled his eyebrows. He even shook his fist in the air and yelled, "I am so angry!"

"Caw! Caw!" said Edgar.

Edgar was angry too.

First it had been the villagers. Then it had
been those cheese-nibbling rats. And then,
when things had finally gone quiet, when
he'd finally picked his violin back up and
set the bow against the strings so that he

could tune it, someone had howled. A long, loud, rolling howl. Then a kitten. A hissing, spitting kitten. Then there had been a boy with a flute. No, a boy *playing* a flute, and three little monsters all smiling and, and, and . . . *breathing*! Breathing can be very, very loud.

Everything was loud to Baron Von Grump. His own breathing was loud. His hollering, hopping, and stomping was loud. He could barely hear himself think.

With the rats gone, the villagers would move back in. With the villagers back, there would be more smiling, and singing, and gum-chewing, and "good mornings." There would be laughing and breathing and good cheer.

"I am so angry!" roared Baron Von Grump, pacing and stomping around.

See? He was really, really angry.

Think of some time when you were really angry. Think of when you had to go to bed early, or eat lima beans, or clean up your toys *before* you could go out and play. That probably made you angry, right? Well, Baron Von Grump was even angrier than that! Like, a hundred times angrier. Maybe a zillion times.

"Caw! Caw!" said Edgar.

"Stop cawing!" hollered Baron Von Grump. He shook his fist at Edgar and stomped some more.

Edgar's little eyes twinkled mischievously. "Caw?" He flew up to the top rafter and stayed out of Baron Von Grump's way.

"Argh!" yelled Baron Von Grump. He stuffed cotton into his ears and slammed his shutters closed.

That was how angry he was.

CHAPTER
12

THE VILLAGERS, HOWEVER, WERE NOT angry. They were very happy to be back home in their village. They were so happy that they gathered right in the village square, every one of them, from young to old.

There was lots of smiling, lots of sing-ing, and lots of good cheer. There was even lots of gum-chewing. These villagers really liked gum.

After the rats were settled, Franky, Wolfy,

and Vampyra walked Peter back to the village. Everyone was gathered in the square.

"Peter," said the mayor, "you led the rats out of the village. You saved the day! I want to give you a medal."

Peter was proud. "Thank you," he said. "But . . ."

"But what?" said the mayor.

"But I didn't do it alone," said Peter. He called his friends over. "Wolfy, Vampyra, and Franky all helped me. We saved the day together!"

"Don't forget Shadow," said Wolfy.

"Meow," said Shadow.

"But . . . but they're monsters!" said one of the villagers. He hid behind a wagon.

"Monsters are scary," said another villager. She grabbed a pitchfork.

"Don't eat me!" said a third villager. He pulled his hat down over his face.

"They won't eat you," said Peter. "And they're *not* scary. These are nice monsters, and they're my friends. These Junior Monster Scouts helped me find Shadow, and then they helped me lead the rats out of the village."

"Monsters?" said the mayor. *"Helping?"*

"By tooth or wing, by paw or claw, a Junior Monster Scout does it all!" said Vampyra, Franky, and Wolfy all together.

"But they live in the old castle!" said one of the villagers.

"Technically, I live in the mountains *near* the castle," mumbled Wolfy.

"Beyond the Gloomy Woods," said another villager.

"Up past the graveyard!" said a third villager.

"And they're terribly frightening!" said the mayor. "It says so right here!"

He held up a large book. The title was *The Big Book of Scary Monsters*.

"Those are just stories!" said Peter.

"They are?" said the mayor and the villagers.

"Those stories aren't real," said Vampyra.

"They're not?" said the mayor and the villagers.

"We're just like you," said Wolfy. "Maybe just furrier."

"And really quite friendly," said Franky.

"Junior Monster Scouts, you say?" said the mayor.

"That's right," said Vampyra. "We help people."

"And take care of the environment," said Wolfy.

"And learn new things!" said Franky.

The mayor scrunched up his eyebrows. He twisted his mustache. He looked from the book to the monsters, and then back to the book. A smile spread across his face and he tossed the book into a nearby haystack.

"Well, it sounds to me like we need four medals!" declared the mayor.

"Don't forget Shadow," said Franky.

"Meow," said Shadow.

"Five medals," said the mayor.

"Three cheers for the Junior Monster Scouts!" said Peter.

"Hip, hip, hooray!" shouted the villagers. "Hip, hip, hooray! Hip, hip, HOORAY!"

CHAPTER
13

AFTER THE CELEBRATION, WOLFY, VAMPYRA, and Franky said good-bye to Peter and Shadow.

"We have to get home," said Wolfy.

"Tonight is our Junior Monster Scout meeting," said Franky.

"But we'll be sure to visit you!" said Vampyra.

They crossed the covered bridge that led out of the village. They passed the Gloomy

Woods. They climbed the hill where Wolfy had practiced his howling. They marched past the old graveyard and back to Castle Dracula just in time to grab their Junior Monster Scout merit badge sashes and make it to their scout meeting.

"So, what did you do today?" asked Franky's dad, Frankenstein.

Wolfy, Vampyra, and Franky took turns telling about how they had helped Peter find Shadow and about leading the rats out of the village.

"And into my basement," mumbled Dracula.

"That sounds like great teamwork!" said Wolfy's dad, Wolf Man. "I think you three earned your Teamwork Merit Badge!"

70

"Really?" asked Wolfy.

"We did?" asked Franky and Vampyra.

Frankenstein opened the Junior Monster Scout handbook. "You worked together to do something you could not have done individually. Wolfy, you led everyone through the woods to Shadow."

"Vampyra, you flew up and found the branch she was on," said Wolf Man.

"And, Franky, you used your head and your height so that you all could get Shadow out of the tree," said Dracula.

"On top of that, all three of you made a new friend. A human friend. Congratulations, junior monsters," said Frankenstein. He pinned their new badges onto their uniforms.

"One more thing," said Dracula. "Wolfy, that was a great howl. I heard it all the way from the top of my castle!"

"Sounds like someone earned their Howling Merit Badge!" said Wolf Man.

Wolfy and Wolf Man leaned way, way, way back and howled at the moon. Dracula, Frankenstein, Franky, and Vampyra joined in.

"Now let's say the Junior Monster Scout oath," said Frankenstein.

The junior monsters held hands and said together, "I promise to be nice, not scary. To help, not harm. To always try to do my best. I am a monster, but I am not mean. I am a Junior Monster *Scout!*"

CHAPTER

14

BARON VON GRUMP GLARED OUT HIS window. He grumped and he glared. He glared and he grumped.

Edgar perched on his shoulder and glared as well.

"Junior Monster Scouts," he grumbled.

"Caw-caw caw-caw caw," grumbled Edgar.

Baron Von Grump put his eye to his telescope and peered out over the village, over

the covered bridge, beyond the Gloomy Woods, past the old graveyard, and to the top of the hill. There, in the great stone castle, *Dracula's* castle, the monsters were celebrating. They were celebrating how they had foiled him. Him, Baron Von Grump! That would never do.

Why, the monsters were the very reason Baron Von Grump had never been recognized for his musical talent! Ever since that day when he was just a young lad, onstage at the village talent show, prepared to play the song he had practiced over and over and over so that he might win the trophy . . . those meddling monsters had come in and scared everyone. Scared him so much that he'd pulled the bow across the strings in a terrible, earsplitting screech. No one had wanted to hear him play after that. No one would listen.

Oh, how Baron Von Grump hated monsters. He hated monsters *more* than he hated smiling, talking, breathing, "good mornings," or gum-chewing.

"Laugh now, you pesky monsters," he growled. "You may have won this round, but you have not seen the last of Baron Von Grump!"

"Caw! Caw!" said Edgar.

Baron Von Grump pulled his shutters closed . . . right onto his telescope. The telescope spun around and slapped into his big, bushy, black eyebrows. Baron Von Grump fell back onto the floor with a loud THUMP.

"I meant to do that," he said, rubbing his eyebrows.

JUNIOR MONSTER SCOUT
· HANDBOOK ·

The Junior Monster Scout oath:

I promise to be nice, not scary. To help, not harm.

To always try to do my best. I am a monster, but

I am not mean. I am a Junior Monster Scout!

Junior Monster Scout mottos:

By paw or claw, by tooth or wing, Junior Monster Scouts can do anything!

Never say "never" when friends work together!

By tooth or wing, by paw or claw, a Junior Monster Scout does it all!

Junior Monster Scout laws:

Be Kind—A scout treats others the way they want to be treated.

Be Friendly—A scout is open to everyone, no matter how different they are.

Be Helpful—A scout goes out of their way to do good deeds for others . . . without expecting a reward.

Be Careful—A scout thinks about what they say or do *before* they do it.

Be a Good Listener—A scout listens to what others have to say.

Be Brave—A scout does what is right, even if they are afraid, and a scout makes the right decisions . . . even if no one else does.

Be Trustworthy—A scout does what they say they will do, even if it is difficult.

Be Loyal—A scout is a good friend and will always be there for you when you need them.

Junior Monster Scout badges in this book:

Flying Merit Badge

Howling Merit Badge

Teamwork Merit Badge

· ACKNOWLEDGMENTS ·

Much like Doctor Frankenstein, standing before his creation, I want to shout, "It's alive!" For this book and this series are very much alive. But it would not be so without some amazing people who have encouraged, supported, guided, and believed in me along the way. Without them, this book would not be in your hands, and I might just be another mad scientist with an even madder idea.

To my wife, my love, my best friend, Jess—together, we have built the life we always wanted; a life filled with love, writing, and adventure. You inspire me. You challenge me. You encourage and celebrate me, and I know that I have been able to accomplish what I have accomplished so far because of your love and support. I'm glad we're not both vampires, because our mortality makes every moment count. I love you and I am so grateful to have you by my side.

Linda—thanks for your vision and for seeing the potential in these books. I appreciate you challenging me to grow my idea.

Karen—you are a rock star! I am beyond lucky to have such an insightful, supportive, and visionary editor. These books howl at the moon because of you. Thank you for believing in me, for loving my stories, and for taking me under your wing. I cannot wait to see what else we do!

Mom—remember that time we were watching *The Fog*, in Pittsburgh, and you asked me to go outside *in the* FOG and check on the dog? Remember when you and Dad tried to make me go in that crazy haunted Brigantine Castle? Well, thanks, I'm scarred (joking). But seriously, thanks for always feeding me books, for taking me to the library, for encouraging my imagination. It was more important than you'll probably ever realize. Dad, thanks for always working hard to provide for us and for letting me chase dragons . . . even when you didn't understand.

To the late George Romero—thank you for bringing the walking dead into mainstream media culture. And thank you for taking me and Cam to see *Empire Strikes Back* and for dinner. You encouraged a young mind to pursue his passion for storytelling and for monsters.

To the late Gary Gygax—thanks for Dungeons & Dragons. Your game (and a thousand others since) developed a passion for storytelling in me from when I was ten years old and sat, spellbound, listening to local teens battling skeletons in a damp, subterranean tomb.

Kathi Appelt, Sharon Darrow, Tom Birdseye, Amy King, and Lisa John-Clough—you taught me so much about my writing, about the craft, about myself. I will forever be indebted to you.

To my Allies in Wonderland—thank you

86

for your friendship and for sharing this crazy writing life. We have read, laughed, cried, and created together. We have supported one another. We're all mad here.

To my VCFA family—you are magical people in a magical place. You changed my life. Thank you.

To my SNC family—I love you all. I never thought I could find a place that would fill the hole left by Vermont. I didn't . . . I found something else entirely: a writer's paradise where my heart sings by being around each and every one of you. I am honored and proud to be a part of such an amazing program, inspired by the talented students, and humbled by the masterful faculty. Brian, thank you for making me a part of your magic and for your friendship. Shannon, thank you for making me feel like a needed and integral part of our program.

Eric, I value your friendship so very much and I look forward to writing, creating, and gaming together. Funny when you find a kindred spirit in the middle of life.

Pablo, my brother—thank you for standing by me from the beginning. For your friendship, your love, and always looking out for Jess and me. And hey, thanks for marrying us, Padre Cartaya!

Becca, Josh, Lena, and Maddie—wow, just wow. So much love and thanks for truly being there. For embracing me and loving me and being my family. Thank you. You'll never know how much your kindness has meant. I love you! 10-3 club!

To our amazing children, Zachary, Ainsley, Shane, Logan, Braeden, and Sawyer—I love you all more than you can imagine. Thank you for not grumbling too much when we pulled you to all of those signings and events and book festivals. You've all been so wonderful in this crazy writing life that Jess and I have chosen. I know it has not always been easy, but thank you.

To Donna and Erica—thanks for your insight and great feedback. It's nice to have a smart, supportive, honest, and fun critique group!

To the Frenchtown community—as I write this, we are about a month from the tragic fire that destroyed our home and two beloved businesses. In the midst of this chaos, of losing everything we had (except our lives and computers), you rallied around us and provided everything from kind words and hugs, to clothes and toothbrushes, to food and a place to stay. You supported us. You loved us. You rallied around us and made the nightmare manageable. Without you, I'm not sure I could have finished my revisions on time, let alone functioned like a normal human being. So thank you all, especially you, Caroline. You are a treasured friend and The Book Garden will always be a special place for us. Kandy, the Art Yard, Brad, Ben, Rosella, Carolyn, The United Way,

Peter, Dawn, and a hundred other people I may have neglected to mention but have not forgotten, thank you!

And to my brother, Jack, who would have been in his twenties now. Who laughed hysterically every time I read *Fox in Socks* faster than humanly possible, who taught me to appreciate life—every fleeting, fragile moment of it—I love you. You are not forgotten. You have never been forgotten and I love you, little brother. I miss you.

One final thanks goes out to all of the teachers, librarians, and parents who go out of their way to encourage creativity and foster a love of reading. It was a Young Authors' Day in elementary school, a one-day series of workshops designed to inspire and encourage young creative writers, that had me convinced I wanted to be an author "when I grew up"; that helped me believe that I *could* be an author when "I grew up." Whether or not I actually grew up is up for debate, but I am an author. I did it. And you helped me believe I could. I thank those of you who do the same today for the writers of tomorrow. They need you. We need them.

FIND OUT WHAT HAPPENS IN
CRASH! BANG! BOO!

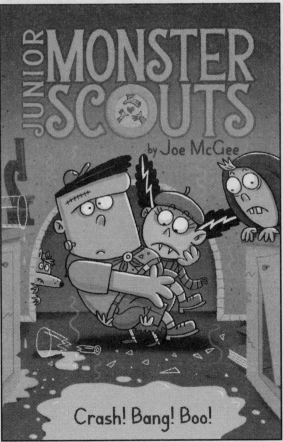

"COME ON, FRANKY!" SAID VAMPYRA. "WE'RE missing all the fun!"

"It sounds like a howling good time!" said Wolfy.

"One more bolt to tighten," said Franky. "There! Now my windup monster is all ready for the village's first ever Monster Mash competition!"

The villagers had been so thankful for the Junior Monster Scouts helping them before, that the mayor insisted the Junior Monster Scouts join them for the village's birthday celebration. To show the Junior Monster Scouts that the villagers were no longer afraid of the monsters (it had all been a big misunderstanding), the mayor declared a special contest: a Monster Mash competition. Whoever created the coolest, the craziest, the most wonderful windup monster would win the first place ribbon and a hand-carved cuckoo clock, made by none other than the mayor himself!

Franky set his wrench down and stepped back. His windup mechanical monster hopped up and down, clapping its claws and waving its tentacles.

"That looks great, Franky!" said Wolfy.

"First place ribbon, here I come," said Franky. "That cuckoo clock will look great in my room!"

"Ribbon, schmibbon," said Vampyra. "Party, here I come!"

"I can smell the popcorn from all the way up here!" said Wolfy.

"Smell it all you want," said Franky. "I plan on *tasting* it! Oh, sweet butter, delicious salt . . ."

He closed his eyes and spun in a circle.

"Not if I get there first and eat it all!" teased Vampyra. She flipped her cape around herself and turned into a bat.

Vampyra, Wolfy, and Franky flew, ran, and charged down the road away from Dracula's Castle, hooting, hollering, and howling. They were going to a party tonight, and they were very excited.

Parties are very fun. And birthday parties are even *more* fun. Only, this birthday party was not for just one person. . . . It was for the entire village! The village was one hundred fifty years old today, and they were having a great big birthday party. One hundred fifty is a lot of years, and so there was a lot of celebrating.

Do you know who was *not* celebrating? Do you know who did not like the *pop, pop, POP* of the popcorn machine? Or the bright lights strung from the tents and buildings? Or the marching band? Or the merry-go-round? Or the sugary scent of fresh birthday cake?

That's right . . . Baron Von Grump. He did not like any of those things.

"Caw! Caw!"

And neither did Edgar, his pet crow.

Baron Von Grump folded his arms. He scrunched his big, black, bushy eyebrows. He glared out his window from the top of the rickety Old Windmill.

"Merry-go-round," he muttered. "There's nothing *merry* about it!"

He picked up his violin and set the bow to the strings, but when he tried to play, the popcorn POPPED!

He tried again. *Pop-pop-POP!* Then the music of the merry-go-round spun round and round, right in through his window.

He marched to the other side of the room,

took a deep breath, set the bow to the strings, and . . . *Pop-pop-POP!* Merry-go-round music. *BOOM-BOOM-BOOM* and trumpets trumpeting, horns blaring as the marching band marched through the village.

"Noise, noise, noise, NOISE!" he bellowed.

A long, high-pitched whistling sounded outside his window, and before he could close the shutters, a single firecracker landed inside his room.

"This is the last—"

POP! BANG! WHIZ!

"Caw!" said Edgar, flapping straight out the window.

"Straw," grumbled Baron Von Grump, collapsing into his chair.

Looking for another great book?
Find it
IN THE MIDDLE.

Fun, fantastic books for kids in the in-beTWEEN age.

IntheMiddleBooks.com

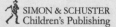